Photography of cut-paper illustrations by Studio One

For my dad, Bill Clements,
who has always shared his workshop, his love, everything
—A.C.

For Ingrid and Michele
—D.W.

Clarion Books. ✣ a Houghton Mifflin Company imprint. ✣ 215 Park Avenue South, New York, NY 10003. ✣ Text copyright © 1999 by Andrew Clements. ✣ Illustrations copyright © 1999 by David Wisniewski. ✣ The text type for this book is set in 17/21-point Guardi bold. ✣ The illustrations for this book are executed in watercolor and Color-Aid cut papers. ✣ All rights reserved. ✣ For information about permission to reproduce selections from this book, write to Permissions, Houghton Mifflin Company, 215 Park Avenue South, New York, NY 10003. ✣ Printed in the USA.
LIBRARY OF CONGRESS CATALOGING-IN-PUBLICATION DATA.
Clements, Andrew, 1949–   Workshop / by Andrew Clements ; illustrated by David Wisniewski.   p.   cm.
Summary: Describes, in rhyming text and illustrations, the characteristics of tools commonly found in most toolboxes.
ISBN 0-395-85579-9   1. Tools—Juvenile literature. 2. Workshops—Juvenile literature.   [1. Tools.]   I. Wisniewski, David, ill. II. Title.   TJ1195C57   1999   621.9—dc21   97-48534   CIP   AC   BVG   10   9   8   7   6   5   4   3   2   1

WORKSHOP

Written by **Andrew Clements** ✦ Illustrated by **David Wisniewski**

CLARION BOOKS ✦ *New York*

Ruler

Ruler knows how long and wide and deep and high.
Ruler never guesses.
Ruler knows.

Axe

Axe is a chopper, a splitter, a sudden rusher.
Axe finds the board that hides in the log.
Axe is the great divider.

Saw

Saw is a biter.
Tooth after tooth,
saw rips away by bits.
Saw turns boards to dust.

Hammer

Hammer is a hitter, a beater, a pounder, a nailer.
Hammer moves, whack by thump by thud.
Hammer keeps swinging.

Anvil

Anvil is hard.
Anvil waits for hammer.
Anvil is below, hammer above.
Whatever comes between is changed.
Anvil is not moved.

Grinder

Grinder wears away.
The blade, the bolt, the chain—
grinder does not care.
Gnawing with a stony tooth,
grinder spits out sparks.

Chisel

Chisel is a chipper, a nibbler, a digger.
Chisel is a little-by-little shaper of wood and metal,
brick and stone.
Chisel is patient.

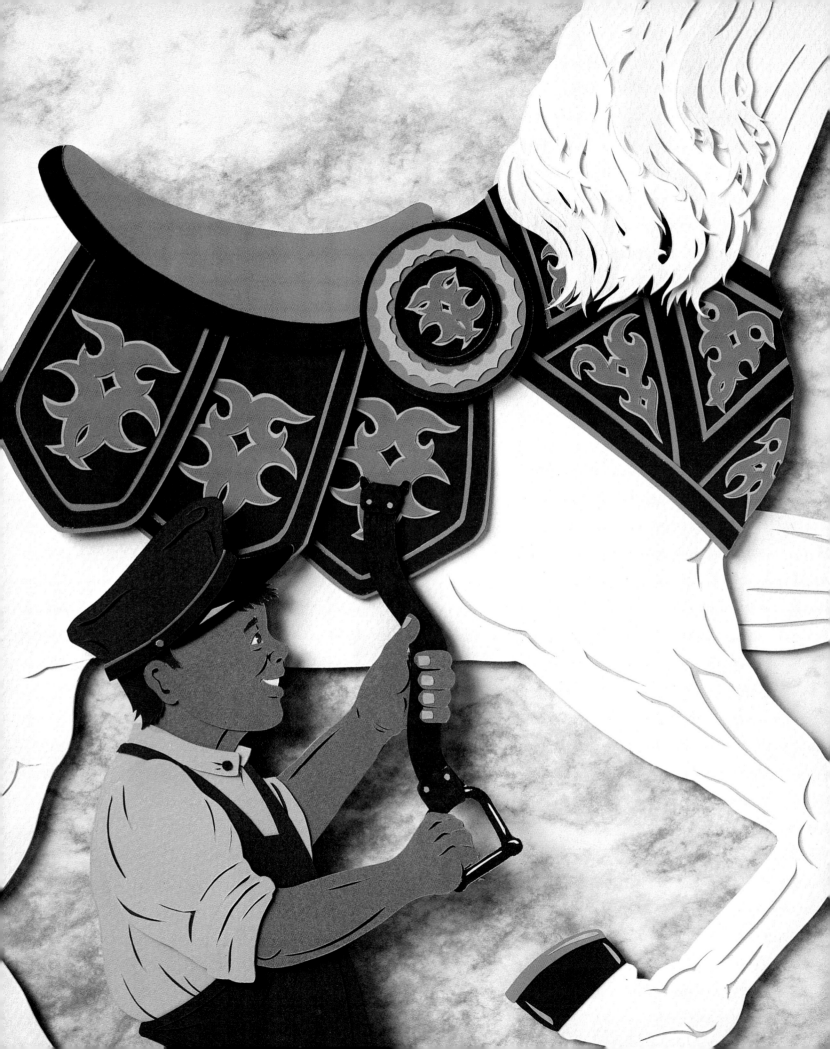

Shears

Shears is a pair.
Shears march sharply into leather, lead, or steel.
Shears cut through and true.

Knife

Knife is a cutter, a slicer, a trimmer.
Knife is thin and edgy.
Knife is just passing through.

Screwdriver

Screwdriver follows screw, servant and master.
Driving in, drawing out, screwdriver turns and turns again.
Alone, screwdriver is a dull chisel.
Alone, screw rusts.
Screwdriver is a partner.

Drill

Drill spins in.
Drill finds the center.
Drill makes room for itself.

Pliers

Pliers pinch and pull.
Pliers grip—long, strong fingers.
Pliers hold tight.

Wrench

Wrench turns the nut.
Wrench turns the pipe.
Wrench loosens, wrench tightens.
Wrench wrestles metal.

Toolbox

Toolbox carries tools away.
Toolbox remembers.
Toolbox carries tools home.
Workshop is home.